Betty

ATOMIC COMICS

Galactic Issue 2

X-5

Grosset & Dunlap

GROSSET & DUNLAP
Published by the Penguin Group

Penguin Group (USA) Inc., 375 Hudson Street, New York, New York 10014, U.S.A. · Penguin Group (Canada), 90 Eglinton Avenue East, Toronto, Ontario, Canada M4P 2Y3 (a division of Pearson Penguin Canada Inc.) · Penguin Books Ltd, 80 Strand, London WC2R 0RL, England · Penguin Ireland, 25 St Stephen's Green, Dublin 2, Ireland (a division of Penguin Books Ltd) · Penguin Group (Australia), 250 Camberwell Road, Camberwell, Victoria 3124, Australia (a division of Pearson Australia Group Pty Ltd) · Penguin Books India Pvt Ltd, 11 Community Centre, Panchsheel Park, New Delhi - 110 017, India · Penguin Group (NZ), Cnr Airborne and Rosedale Roads, Albany, Auckland 1310, New Zealand (a division of Pearson New Zealand Ltd) · Penguin Books (South Africa) (Pty) Ltd, 24 Sturdee Avenue, Rosebank, Johannesburg 2196, South Africa

Penguin Books Ltd, Registered Offices: 80 Strand, London WC2R 0RL, England

Library of Congress Control Number: 2005017538

ISBN 0-448-44003-2
10 9 8 7 6 5 4 3 2 1

Purrsy versus Harold? This is not good!

Cut it out, Purrsy. Leave that poor frog alone!

Harold, do not go out that window. I repeat, *do not* go out that window!

Ribbit!

Outside, Betty searched
high and low for Harold.

In just a few moments,
Betty became...

Atomic Betty!

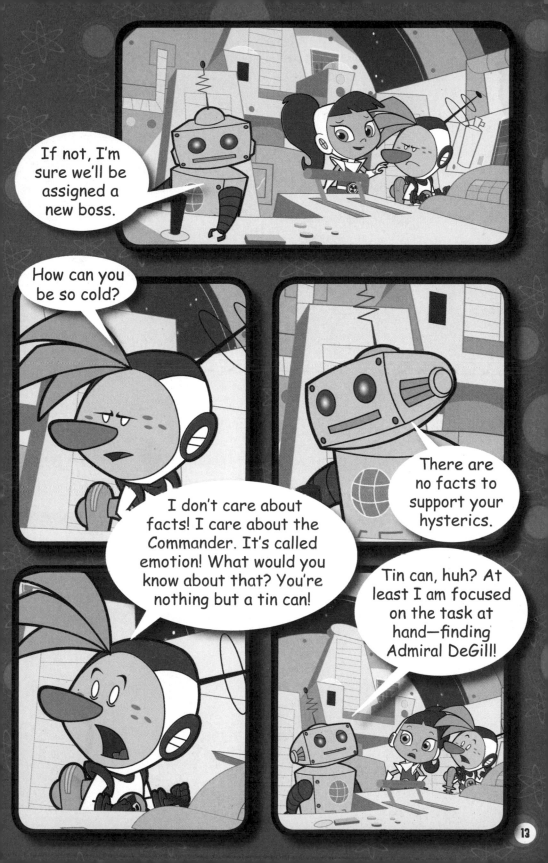

While Betty and Sparky put on their disguises, X-5 slipped off to the East Mechanical Repair and Recalibration Dock.

PLOP!

SQUISH!

SSSLURP!

Yowch! Those estheticians are . . . terrible!

That's because they're imposters! Look at their uniforms! If I'm not mistaken . . .

Betty and Sparky zipped down the hall.

It's the real employees!

And that's a Radooshian Mind Control orb. Don't look at it!

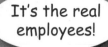

One hit from my Blastration Ray and the mind control orb will be history!

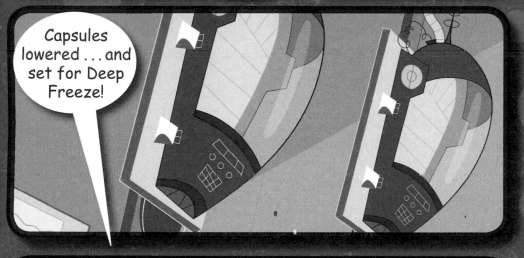
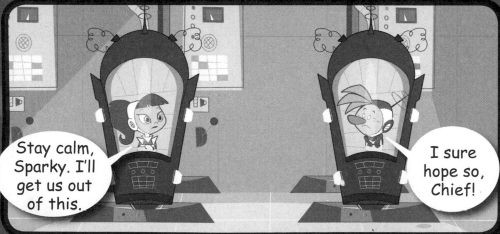

A well-placed kick from Betty knocked both thugs out of business...

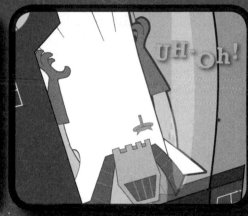

and into the ice capsules! 37

But Betty's troubles weren't over yet.

While Sparky and X-5 duked it out, Betty faced off against Maximus's entire robot army.

Mmm, I could really go for a glass of carrot-pineapple-blurgbug juice right about now.

I had that for breakfast. I want a Pringonian protein smoothie!

Where are you going? Halt! I command you!

Juice break. Union rules.

Saved by the bell!

Nothing can stop me now!

Except that!

54

zZzoooOoMMMMMMm!

CRASH!

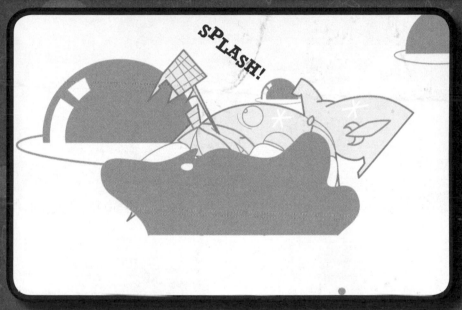

Betty splashed the waterbugs on the windowsill to lure Harold back— just as Purrsy pounced!

Uh-oh! Purrsy's going to need a bath now—and he won't like that one bit.